THIS
WALKER BOOK

BELONGS TO

_____

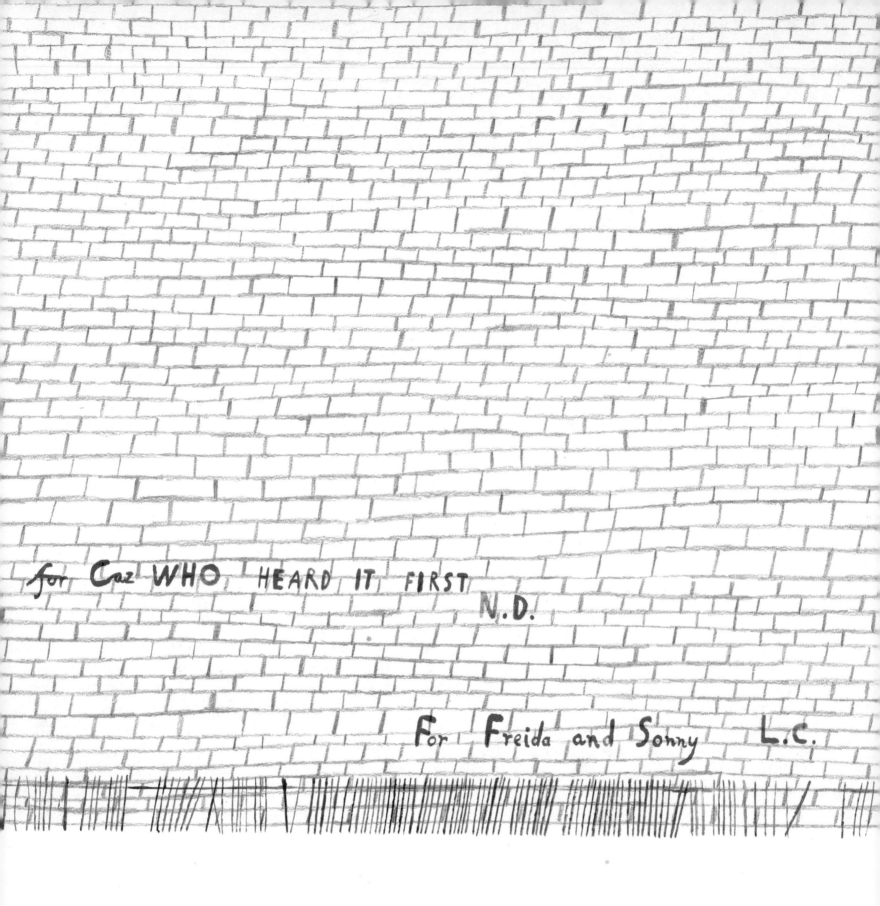

for Caz WHO HEARD IT FIRST

N.D.

For Freida and Sonny   L.C.

THE PROMISE

First published 2013
by Walker Books Ltd
87 Vauxhall Walk, London SE11 5HJ

This edition published 2014

2 4 6 8 10 9 7 5 3

Text © 2013 Nicola Davies
Illustrations © 2013 Laura Carlin

This book has been typeset in Rockwell

Printed in China

British Library Cataloguing in
Publication Data: a catalogue
record for this book is available
from the British Library

ISBN 978-1-4063-5559-8

www.walker.co.uk

WALKER BOOKS
AND SUBSIDIARIES

LONDON · BOSTON · SYDNEY · AUCKLAND

THE
PROMISE
NICOLA DAVIES

ILLUSTRATED BY LAURA CARLIN

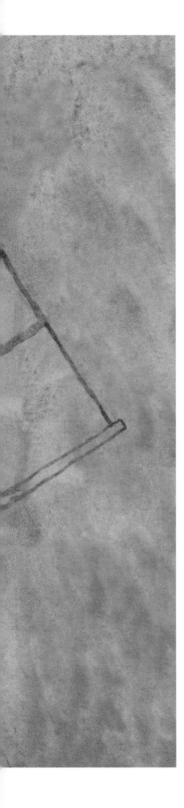

When I was young I lived in a city

that was mean and hard and ugly.

Its streets were dry as dust,

cracked by heat and cold,

and never blessed with rain.

A gritty, yellow wind blew constantly,

scratching round the buildings

like a hungry dog.

Nothing grew.   Everything was broken.   No one ever smiled.

The people had grown as mean and hard and ugly as their city,
and I was mean and hard and ugly too.

I lived by stealing from those who had almost as little as I did.

My heart was as shrivelled as the dead trees in the park.

And then, one night,

I met an old lady down a dark street.

She was frail and alone, an easy victim.

Her bag was fat and full,

but when I tried to snatch it from her,

she held on with the strength of heroes.

To and fro we pulled that bag until at last she said,

"If you promise to plant them, I'll let go."

What did she mean? I didn't know or care,

I just wanted the bag, so I said,

"All right, I promise."

She loosened her grip at once and smiled at me.

I ran off without a backward look,
thinking of the food and money in her bag.

But when I opened it ...
there were only acorns.
I stared at them,
so green, so perfect
and so many,
and understood

the promise

I had made.
I held a forest in my arms,
and my heart was changed.

I forgot the food and money.

And for the first time in my life I felt lucky,

rich beyond my wildest dreams.

I slept with the acorns for my pillow,

my head full of leafy visions.

And in the morning I began to keep

my promise.

I planted beside roads, on roundabouts,

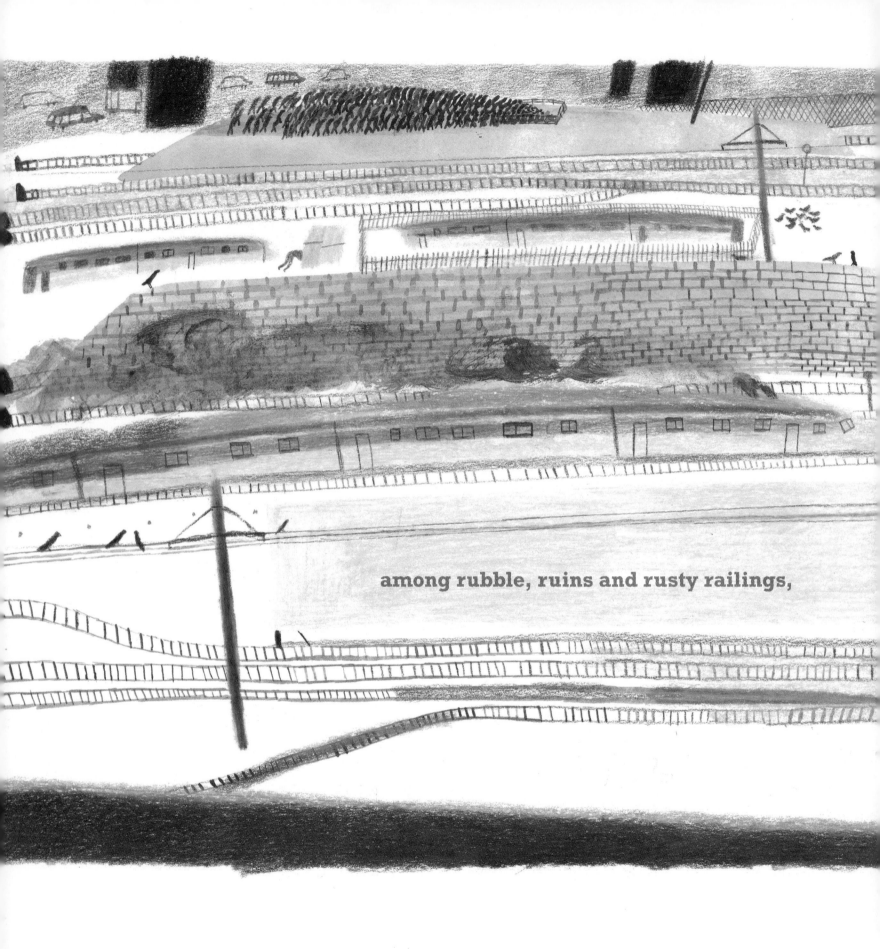

among rubble, ruins and rusty railings,

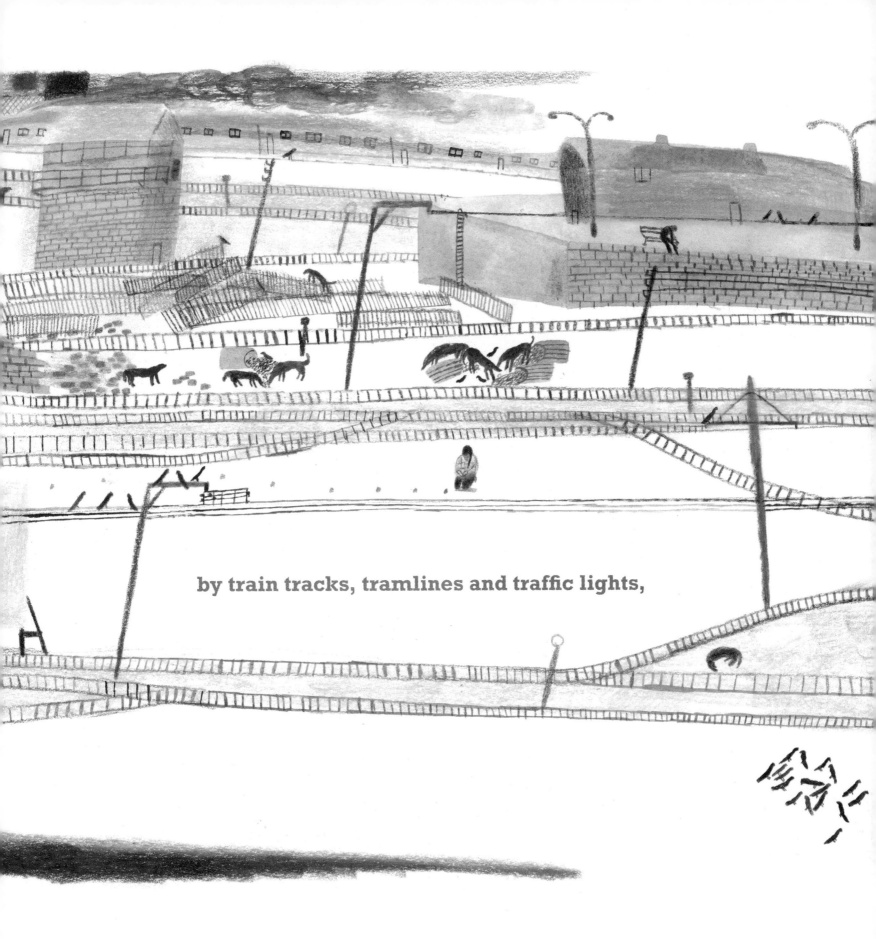

by train tracks, tramlines and traffic lights,

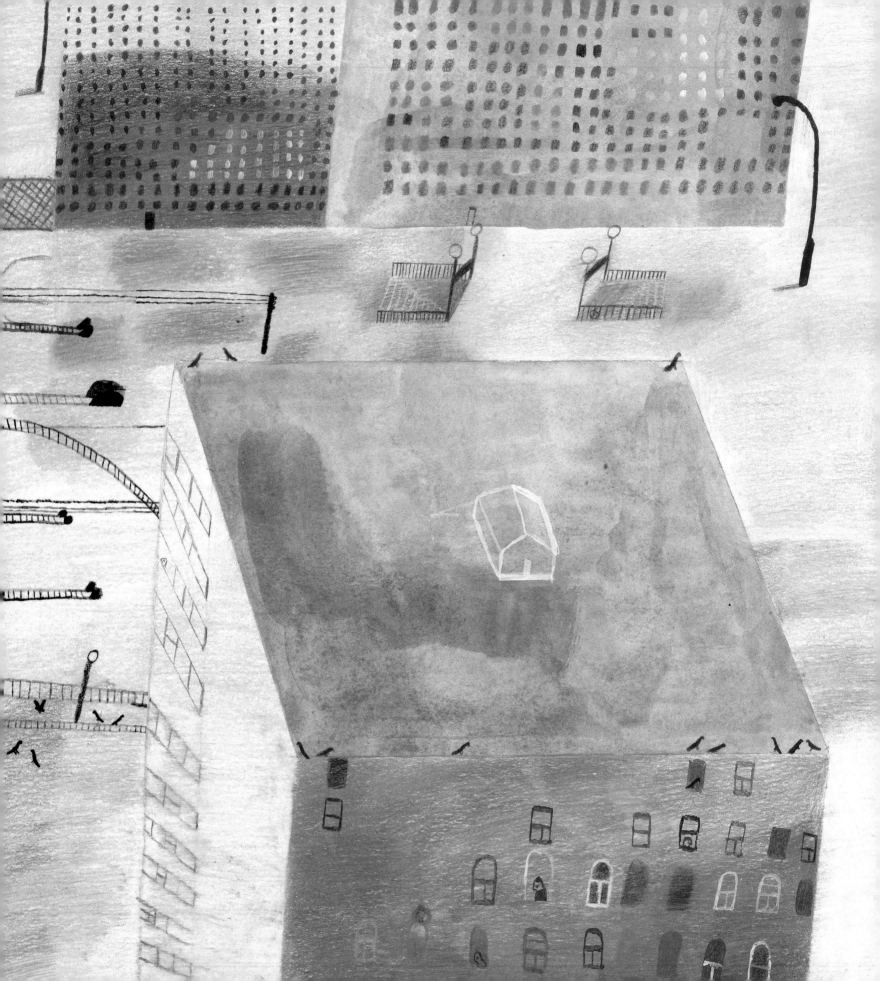

in abandoned parks

and gardens laced with broken glass,

behind factories and shopping malls,

at bus stops, cafés, blocks of flats.

I pushed aside the mean and hard and ugly

and I planted, planted, planted.

Nothing changed at first.

The gritty wind still scratched the parched, cracked streets.

The people scowled and scuttled to their homes like cockroaches.

But slowly, slowly, slowly shoots of green began to show…

TREES!
First here

and there,

then everywhere.

People came onto the streets to see.

They touched the leaves in wonder,
and they smiled.

They took tea together
by the tiny trees.

They talked and laughed ...

and pretty soon they were planting too. Trees and flowers,

fruit and vegetables, in parks and gardens, on balconies and rooftops.

Green spread through the city like a song,

breathing to the sky, drawing down the rain like a blessing.

But by then I was already far away,

planting in another sad and sorry city ...

and another ...

and another ...

and another.

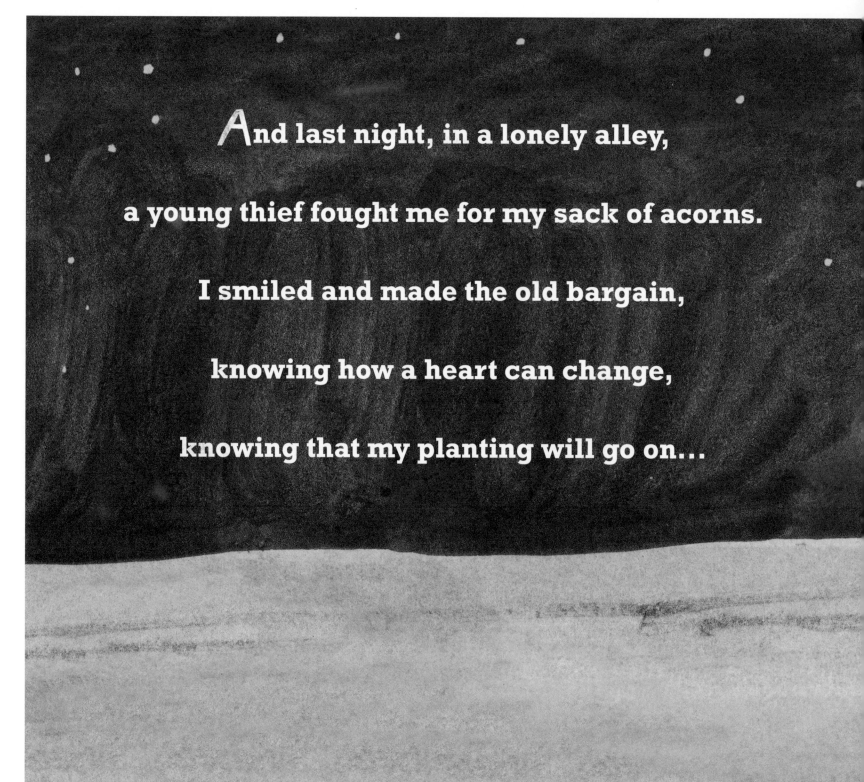

And last night, in a lonely alley,

a young thief fought me for my sack of acorns.

I smiled and made the old bargain,

knowing how a heart can change,

knowing that my planting will go on...

Nicola Davies

is an award-winning author, whose many books for children include
A First Book of Nature, Ice Bear, Big Blue Whale, Bat Loves the Night
and the Heroes of the Wild series. Underlying all her writing
is the belief that our relationship with nature is essential, and that now,
more than ever, we need to renew that relationship.
Nicola lives in Abergavenny, Wales.

Laura Carlin

is a graduate of the Royal College of Art and the winner of several awards,
including the V&A Book Illustration Award for *The Iron Man* by Ted Hughes.
Her work has featured in *Vogue,* the *Guardian* and *The New York Times*.
Laura lives in London.

Look out for:

ISBN 978-1-4063-4916-0   ISBN 978-1-4063-2957-5

Available from all good booksellers

www.walker.co.uk